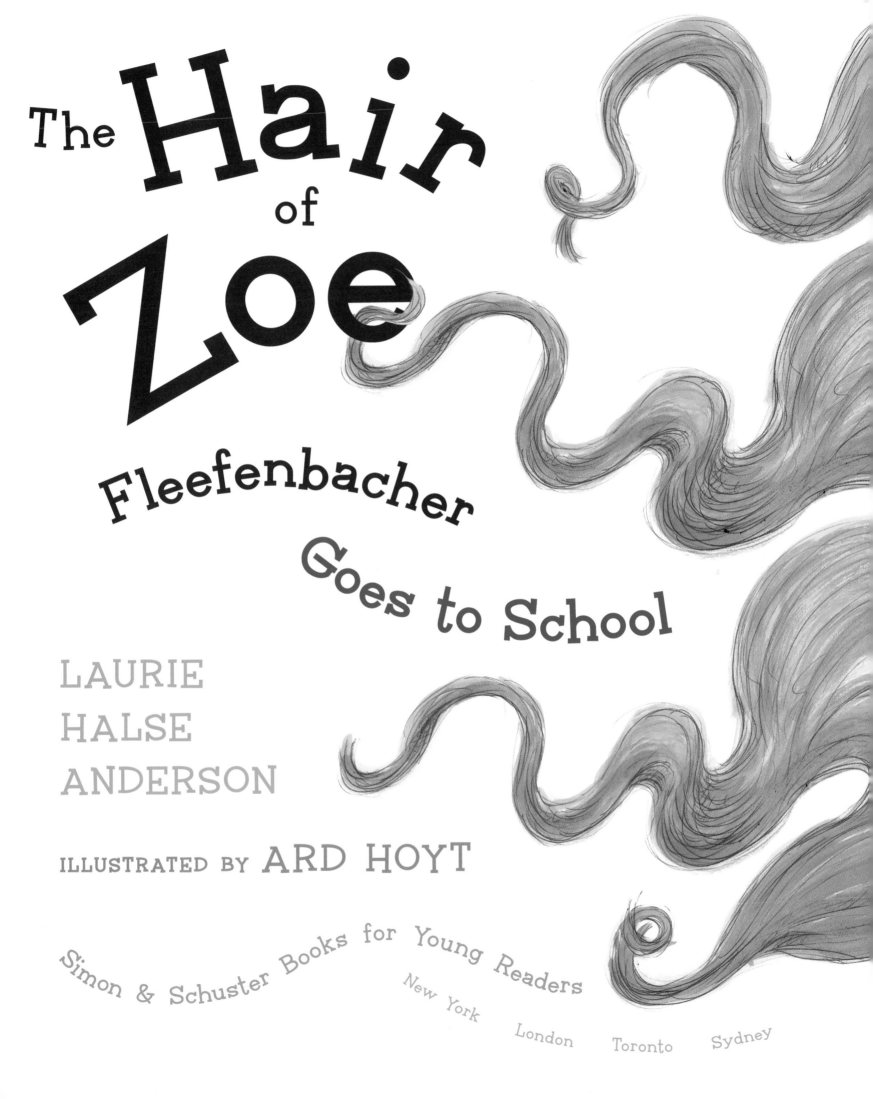

The Hair of Zoe

Fleefenbacher Goes to School

LAURIE
HALSE
ANDERSON

ILLUSTRATED BY ARD HOYT

Simon & Schuster Books for Young Readers

New York   London   Toronto   Sydney

ZOE FLEEFENBACHER
had one blue eye and one green eye,
and bright red hair that went on . . .

. . . forever.

When Zoe was a baby, she needed two strollers
and two cribs and two high chairs. One for
Zoe Fleefenbacher and one for Zoe's hair.

When she was two years old, Zoe's hair learned how to open the cookie jar.

At three, her hair could turn on the TV, pour a glass of juice, pet the cat, and play on the computer—all at the same time.

At four, it
learned to fly.

Mom and Dad Fleefenbacher
threw out the brushes and
combs. The hair of their
Zoe was wild and beautiful.

It was her sail, her kite,
her flag.

Zoe had Mrs. Brodhag for kindergarten.

Mrs. Brodhag let Zoe's hair pick up the trash,
erase the board, and set the table for snack.
At nap time, the hair was a comfort.

Zoe had Ms. Trisk for first grade.
Ms. Trisk didn't fool around.

"School has rules," she said.
"No wild hair in my class!"

Zoe Fleefenbacher's hair did not listen. When Ms. Trisk wrote on the board, Zoe's hair tickled everybody.

Ms. Trisk sat Zoe in time-out.
Zoe's hair drew all over the walls.

Ms. Trisk took charge of the situation.

Big mistake.

"This must stop!" shouted Ms. Trisk.

"School has rules!"

Ms. Trisk demanded a meeting with *the principal*. Zoe's hair had to wait outside.

The grown-ups agreed. School had rules. That hair had to be tamed.

Zoe tried a ponytail.

It didn't work.

Zoe tried braids.

No good.

Zoe tried scrunchies, barrettes, clips,
headbands, rubber bands, bobby pins,
and duct tape—all at the
same time. The class
held its breath
and . . .

it . . . worked!

The hair stayed under control
during spelling. A scrunchy
broke during math, but
the hair didn't move.

Two barrettes slipped out
during snack time, but
the hair didn't move.

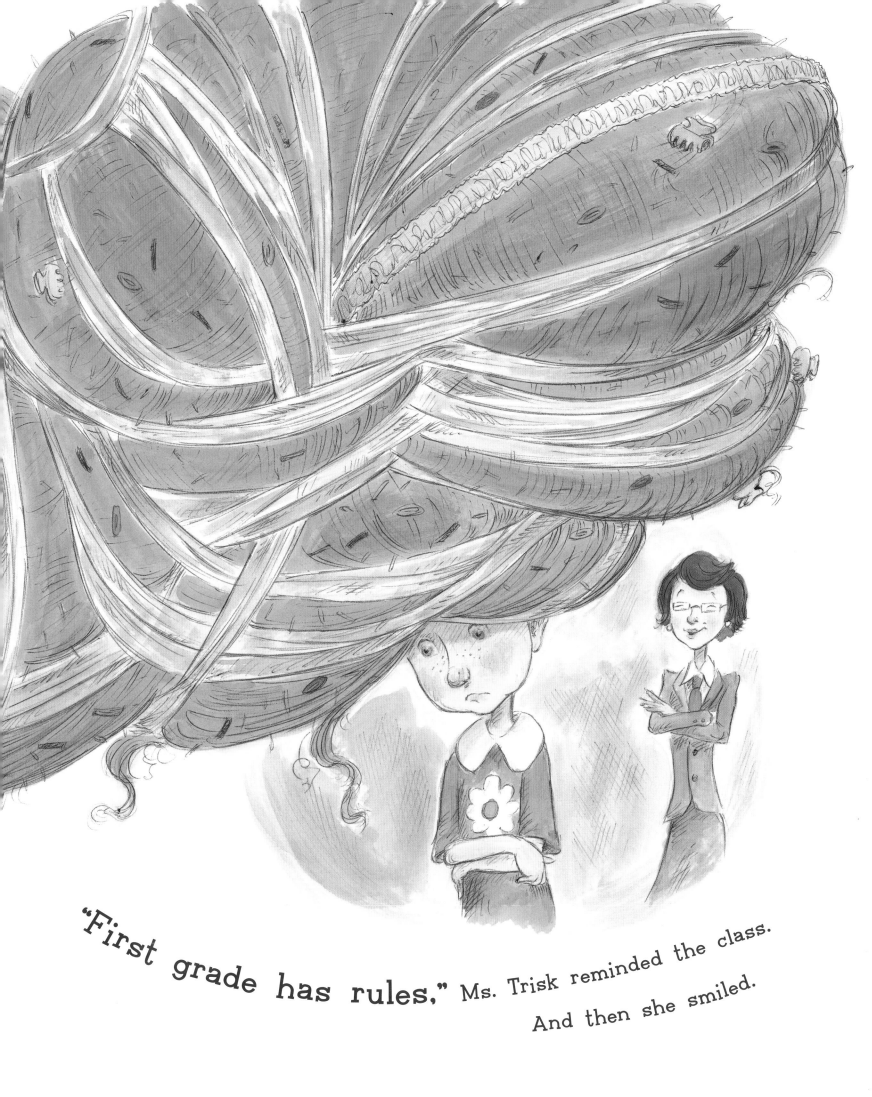

"First grade has rules," Ms. Trisk reminded the class.
And then she smiled.

Zoe couldn't smile. It felt like all the rules in the world were sitting on top of her head.

Ms. Trisk started the science lesson. She held up a ball. "This is the Sun." She held up another ball. "Mercury orbits the Sun." She picked up three other balls. "This is Venus, Mars, and here is the Earth."

She dropped the Earth. The class giggled.

"First grade has rules," Ms. Trisk reminded them. "No giggling."

Zoe lifted her head off the desk.
A bobby pin fell to the floor.
One red strand of hair unfurled.

Ms. Trisk picked up two more
balls. "Pretend that these are
Jupiter and Saturn and that
all the planets are spinning
and orbiting around the Sun."
BAM! BAM! BAM!
Jupiter, Mars, and Venus fell
to the floor and rolled into
the corner.

Ping! Ping! Ping!
Bobby pins rained on the
floor around Zoe.

"Oh, my," said Ms. Trisk.

Snap! Snap! Rubber bands and scrunchies bounced off the ceiling. Barrettes, headbands, and duct tape rocketed through the air. The hair of Zoe Fleefenbacher exploded into the classroom.

"I can help!" Zoe hollered. "I know how to do it!"

Whap! Pop! Whoosh!

The class gasped. Zoe's hair was loose!
The kids grabbed their crayons and hid their
scissors. Ms. Trisk dived for the gerbils' cage.

Zoe smoothed her hair and raised her hand. "Please, Ms. Trisk," she said. "I want to help. Can I try?"

Ms. Trisk nodded.

Zoe's hair picked up Mercury, Venus, the Earth, Mars, Jupiter, Saturn, Uranus, Neptune, and the Sun.

SUN

"The planets spin . . . ," said Ms. Trisk.

Zoe's hair spun the planets.

". . . as they orbit the Sun."

Zoe's hair twirled the planets along their paths.

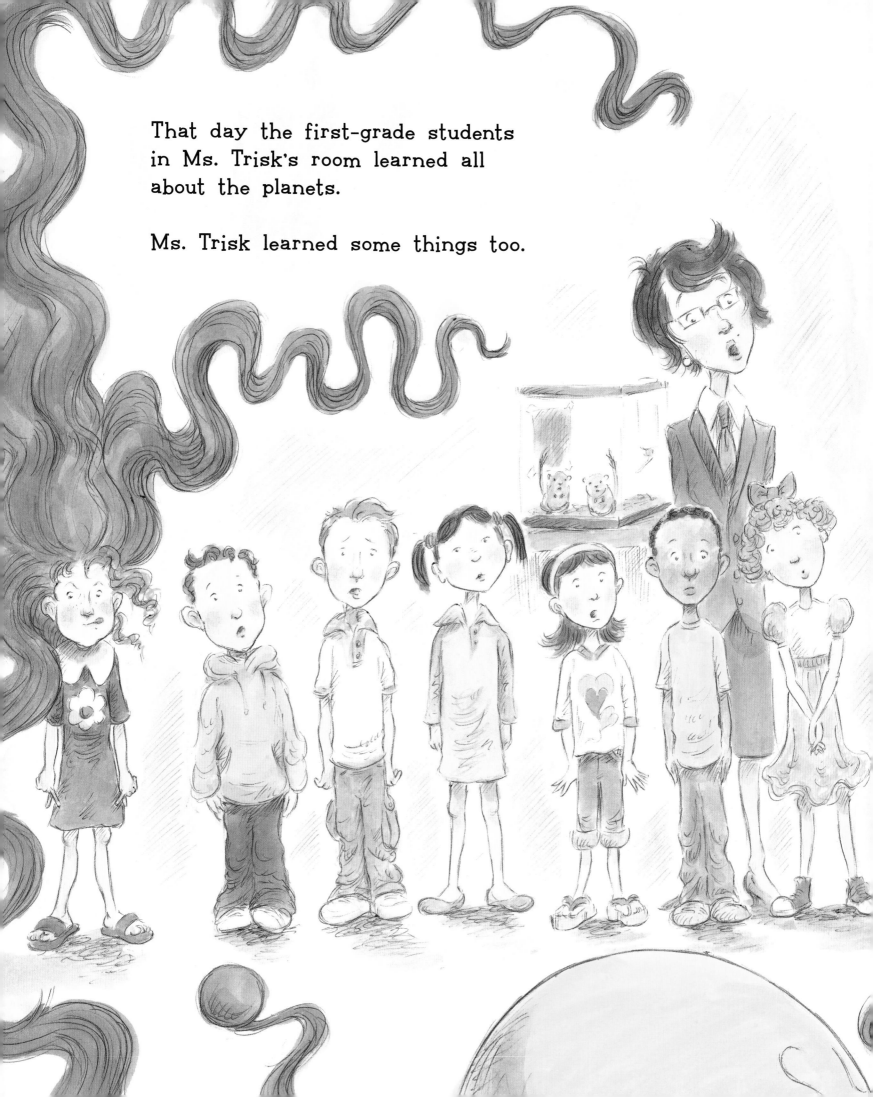

That day the first-grade students in Ms. Trisk's room learned all about the planets.

Ms. Trisk learned some things too.

"My goodness," said Ms. Trisk. "That is some amazing hair. That's helpful hair! That's handy hair!"

Zoe Fleefenbacher had one blue eye and one green eye, and handy, helpful, amazing hair . . .

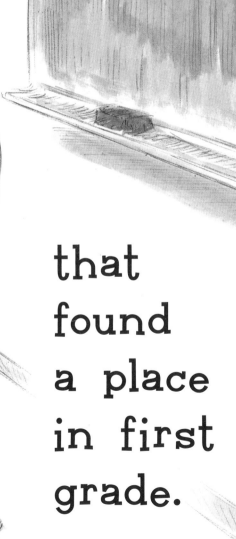

that
found
a place
in first
grade.

This book is dedicated to my daughter,
Meredith Anderson, for being an energetic student
and becoming an understanding teacher.—L. H. A.

To my Grandmother LaPreal, with eternal gratitude for
sharing your love, your home, your stories, and your
nose with me—but most of all for being my friend.
Always your Arizona cowboy—A. H.

ACKNOWLEDGMENTS

I would like to jump up and down and shout "THANK YOU" to the enthusiastic
crew of rule-benders who helped bring Zoe to life: artist, Ard Hoyt; book
designer, Jessica Sonkin; and our irrepressible editor, Kevin Lewis—L. H. A.

SIMON & SCHUSTER BOOKS FOR YOUNG READERS • An imprint of Simon & Schuster Children's
Publishing Division • 1230 Avenue of the Americas, New York, New York 10020 • Text copyright ©
2009 by Laurie Halse Anderson • Illustrations copyright © 2009 by Ard Hoyt • All rights reserved,
including the right of reproduction in whole or in part in any form. • SIMON & SCHUSTER BOOKS FOR
YOUNG READERS is a trademark of Simon & Schuster, Inc. • Book design by Jessica Sonkin • The
text for this book is set in Plumbsky. • The illustrations for this book are rendered in pen and
ink with watercolor on Arches paper. • Manufactured in China • 10 9 8 7 6 5 4 3 2 1 • Library of
Congress Cataloging-in-Publication Data • Anderson, Laurie Halse. • The hair of Zoe Fleefenbacher
goes to school / Laurie Halse Anderson ; illustrated by Ard Hoyt—1st ed. • p. cm. • Summary:
A little girl's talented and untamed hair can open cookie jars and play computer games, much
to the displeasure of her strict first-grade teacher who has rules for everything, including hair.
• ISBN: 978-0-689-85809-3 (hardcover) • [1. Hair—Fiction. 2. Rules (Philosophy)—Fiction.
3. Schools—Fiction. 4. Humorous stories.] I. Hoyt, Ard, ill. II. Title. • PZ7.A54385Hai 2009
• [E]—dc22 • 2007045161